THE GREAT CAT CHASE

By Mercer Mayer

IN MEMORY OF MUSO
WHO WAS EVERYTHING A CAT SHOULD BE

A RAINBIRD PRESS/ J.R. SANSEVERE BOOK

First Rainbird Edition 1994
Printed in Italy
Distributed by Publishers Group West

One day Sarah Jane took Kitty for a ride . . .
but Kitty was not happy.

So Kitty ran away . . .

and hid from Sarah Jane.

"Help! Help!" said Sarah Jane.

"Kitty ran away."

"There's Kitty," said the policeman.

"Here Kitty, Kitty," he said.

But Kitty did not listen.

Kitty ran away. . . .

And everyone followed . . .

Kitty.

"Whoa! Where did Kitty go?"
asked the policeman.

"That way," said Sarah Jane.

"Help me!" said Sarah Jane.

"I'm falling."

Splash went Sarah Jane and the policeman,
just as Kitty came back.

"There goes Kitty!" said Sarah Jane.

Sarah Jane crawled back into the pipe.

And just as she thought,
Kitty was on the other side.

Kitty jumped on the policeman . . .

and then climbed up a tree.

"Oh no!" said Sarah Jane. "Kitty will fall."

"Gotcha!" said the policeman . . .

as he started to . . .

fall.

"Come with me," said Sarah Jane.

"I know just what we need."

"Milk and cookies for everyone!"